PRINCESS CANDY

THE MARSHMALLOW MERMAID

STONE ARCH BOOKS

MINNEAPOLIS   SAN DIEGO

Graphic Sparks are published by Stone Arch Books
151 Good Counsel Drive, P.O. Box 669
Mankato, Minnesota 56002
www.stonearchbooks.com

Library of Congress Cataloging-in-Publication Data

Dahl, Michael.
  The marshmallow mermaid / by Michael Dahl ; illustrated by Jeff Crowther.
    p. cm. -- (Graphic sparks. Princess Candy)
  ISBN 978-1-4342-1588-8 (lib. bdg.)
  1. Graphic novels. [1. Graphic novels. 2. Superheroes--Fiction. 3. Mermaids--
Fiction. 4. Schools--Fiction.] I. Crowther, Jeff, ill. II. Title.
  PZ7.7.D34Mar 2010
  741.5'973--dc22

                                        2009011408

Summary: At Halo Nightly's school, the swimmers are
disappearing from the boys' swim team. No one can
figure it out, until Halo stars investigating. A deadly
mermaid lives in a cave connected to the school
swimming pool. Halo will have to use her special
candy to turn into various underwater
fauna, such as a hammerhead shark
or an octopus, to defeat the
hungry girl-fish!

Creative Director:
Heather Kindseth

Graphic Designer:
Brann Garvey

Printed in the United States of America

PRINCESS CANDY

THE MARSHMALLOW MERMAID

WRITTEN BY
MICHAEL DAHL

ILLUSTRATED BY
JEFF CROWTHER

Midnight Elementary School . . .

The students and teachers have all left the building.

And now, something has left the swimming pool.

15

Later, after classes are done for the day . . .

CREAK!

Maybe if I look around, I can find out what happened to Cody.

SMUNCH!
SMUNCH!

What's that smell?

SNIFF
SNIFF

About The Author

Michael Dahl is the author of more than 200 books for children and young adults. He has won the AEP Distinguished Achievement Award three times for his non-fiction. His Finnegan Zwake mystery series was shortlisted twice by the Anthony and Agatha awards. He has also written the Library of Doom series and the Dragonblood books. He is a featured speaker at conferences around the country on graphic novels and high-interest books for boys.

About The Illustrator

Jeff Crowther has been drawing comics for as long as he can remember. Since graduating from college, Jeff has worked on a variety of illustrations for clients including Disney, Adventures Magazine, and Boy's Life Magazine. He also wrote and illustrated the webcomic Sketchbook and has self-published several mini-comics. Jeff lives in Boardman, Ohio, with his wife, Elizabeth, and their children, Jonas and Noelle.

Glossary

active ingredients (AK-tiv in-GREE-dee-uhnts)—the main items that something is made from

allergic (uh-LUR-jik)—if you are allergic to something, it can cause a reaction, such as a rash, sneezing, or sickness

apartment (uh-PART-muhnt)—rooms inside a larger building that are rented as a home

dreadful (DRED-fuhl)—very bad

gelatin (JEL-uh-tuhn)—a clear substance often used for making jelly or desserts

gush (GUHSH)—to flow quickly in large amounts

gymnasium (jim-NAY-zee-uhm)—a gym, or a large room with equipment for exercises and sports

practical joke (PRAK-tuh-kuhl JOKE)—a prank intended to trick or embarrass someone

whereabouts (WAIR-uh-bouts)—roughly where someone or something is located

MARSHMALLOW MERMAID

SUPER-VILLAIN

Villain Facts

First Appearance
Princess Candy: Marshmallow Mermaid

Real Name.................Mildred Barnacle

Occupation...................Former Student

Height..............................4 feet 7 inches

Weight..........85 pounds (dripping wet)

Eyes...Black

Hair................................Seaweed Green

Special Powers
Ability to travel through water at super-speed; capable of unlimited underwater breathing; super-powerful sweet tooth

While preparing for the Annual Pond Swimming Championships in 1889, young Mildred Barnacle went missing. The sheriff of Midnight searched the town for months, but Mildred was never found. A decade later, workers drained the local wateringhole and built Midnight Elementary in its place. For a hundred years, students passed through the school's doors, unaware of what lay beneath. Then one day, a crack in the swimming pool allowed Mildred to emerge from her watery grave. She had become the slippery and sweet-toothed . . . Marshmallow Mermaid!

AUNT PANDORA'S
PRINCESS PUZZLERS

Q: Who ate the first marshmallows?

A: Believe it or not, ancient Egyptian royalty snacked on marshmallows more than 4,000 years ago.

Q: Where did marshmallows get their funny name?

A: Egyptians made the first marshmallows from "mallow" plants, which are often found in swampy "marshes."

Q: How big was the largest s'more ever made?

A: Built in 2003, the world's largest s'more weighed 1,600 pounds and contained 20,000 toasted marshmallows!

DISCUSSION QUESTION

1. Cody is allergic to marshmallows. Are you allergic to any types of food? If so, how do you deal with your allergy? If not, have you ever met anyone with a food allergy?

2. If Doozie Hiss was captured by the Marshmallow Mermaid, do you think Halo would save her? Why or why not?

3. At the end of the story, Halo escapes the Marshmallow Mermaid. Do you think the evil fish will ever return to Midnight Elementary? Why or why not?

WRITING PROMPTS

1. Pretend your favorite candy could turn you into a superhero. What would your superhero name be? What superpowers would you have? How would you use those powers?

2. Imagine you are the author and write a second part to this story. Does the Marshmallow Mermaid come back? Does Cody win his swim race?

3. Comics and graphic novels are often written and illustrated by two different people. Write a short story, and then give it to a friend to draw the pictures.